I'm Reading About

NORTH DAKOTA

The Peace Garden State!

GALLOPADE

by Carole Marsh

Printed and Manufactured in Peachtree City, GA., USA
www.gallopade.com

Book design: John Hanson

Editorial manager: Janice Baker

North Dakota is a great state.

It is one of a kind.

What makes North Dakota special?

Let's read about it and see!

NATIVE AMERICANS

Who lived in North Dakota first?

Native Americans did!

They moved around to find food.
They hunted for animals to eat.
They fished in North Dakota's rivers.
They gathered fruits and seeds and nuts.

EXPLORERS

The first explorers came to North Dakota in 1738.
They were Frenchmen from the country of Canada.

They were looking for a route
to the Pacific Ocean!

SETTLEMENT

Many settlers came to North Dakota
in the late 1800s.
Several important railroads were built
through North Dakota.
Many people built towns along the railroads.

Fargo was one of the
first towns built along the
Northern Pacific Railway.

Fargo

HARNESS SHOP
GEO. COOPER
HARNESS SHOP.
FARGO
NEWS DEPOT.
CITY
Fargo

STATEHOOD

North Dakota was the 39th state to join the United States of America!

Isn't it great,
to be a state!
I bet North Dakota
could hardly wait!

North Dakota became a state in 1889.

North Dakota

The 39th State

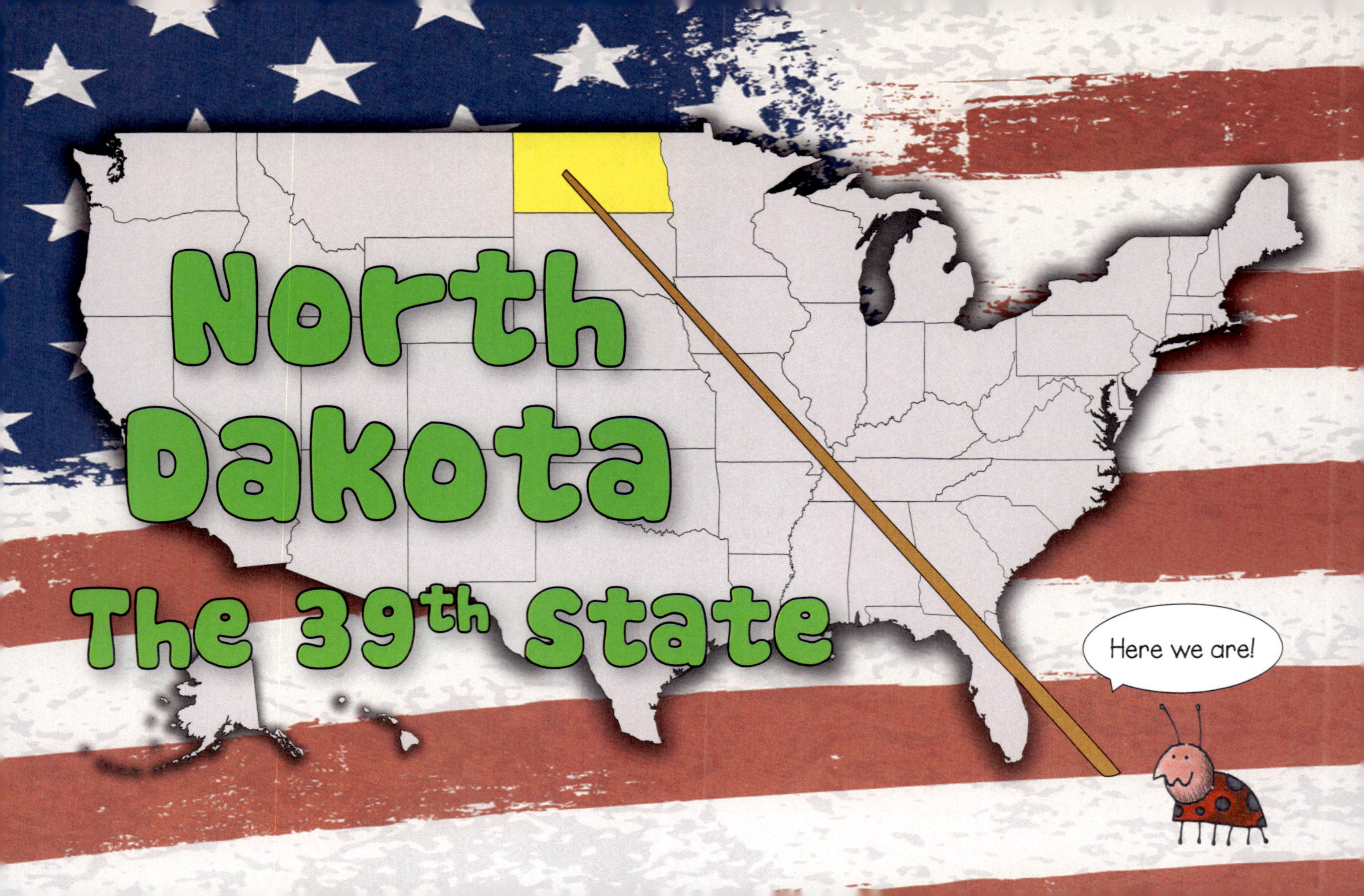

FLAG

I am the state flag.
I was adopted in 1911.

What color am I?
I am blue.

Look at me.
What else do you see?

I fly high over the state of North Dakota!

E PLURIBUS UNUM
NORTH DAKOTA

CAPITAL

Say hello to Bismarck,
the capital city of North Dakota!

There is an important building in Bismarck.
It is the State Capitol.
North Dakota's laws are made there!

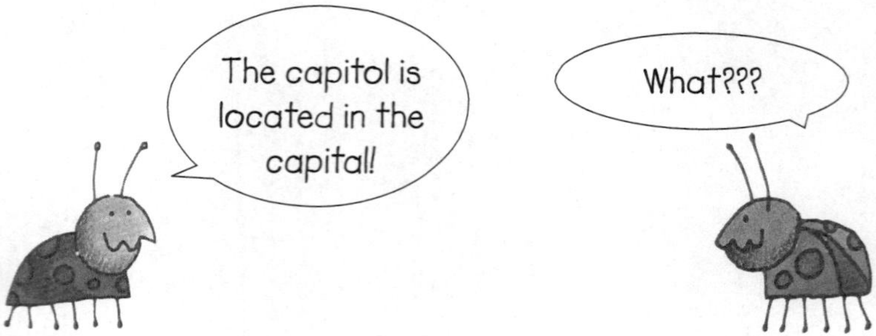

Capitol

SEAL

I am a seal,
but I am not the State Seal.
If I were, I would be very important.
I would be stamped on many official papers.
(Ouch, that might hurt!)

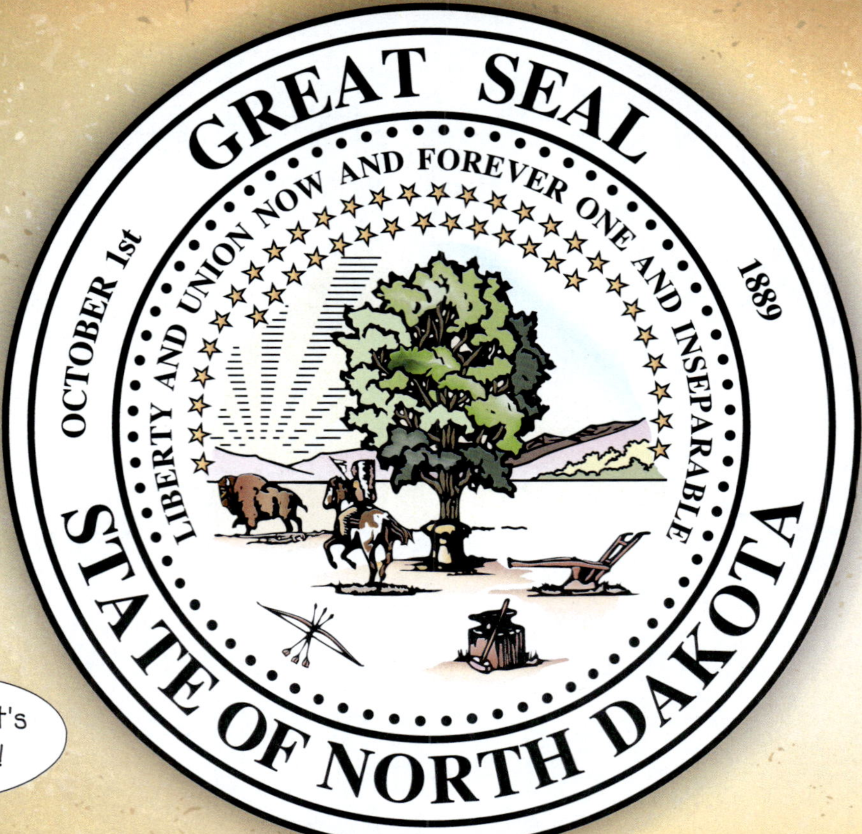
GREAT SEAL
OCTOBER 1st
1889
LIBERTY AND UNION NOW AND FOREVER ONE AND INSEPARABLE
STATE OF NORTH DAKOTA

Now, that's official!

NICKNAME

State nicknames are fun!
State nicknames are great!
They share fun facts
about each state!

North Dakota's nickname is
"The Peace Garden State."

North Dakota has a beautiful Peace Garden!
It is planted on the border
of North Dakota and Canada.

The Peace Garden State

BORDERS

Look at North Dakota.
North Dakota is in a region called "the Midwest."

North Dakota borders three other states.
It also borders the country of Canada.
Find North Dakota and its neighbors on the map!

Dakota is a Native American word that means "friend."

Borders

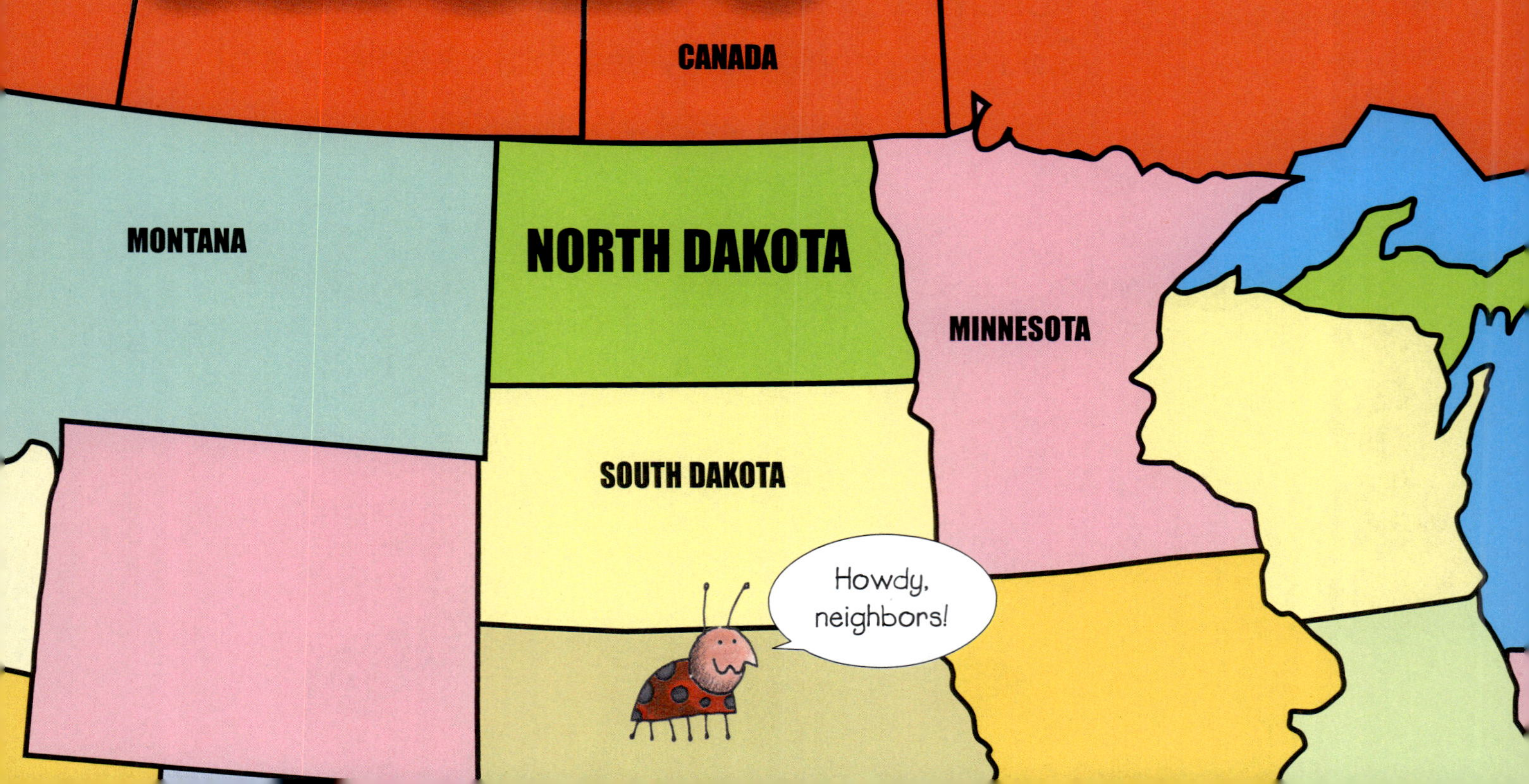
CANADA
MONTANA
NORTH DAKOTA
MINNESOTA
SOUTH DAKOTA
Howdy, neighbors!

COUNTIES

North Dakota is divided into 53 counties.
Counties are a form of local government.
Counties provide services that people need!
Those services include:

Schools **Parks** **Libraries** **Police** **Firefighters** **and More!**

Counties

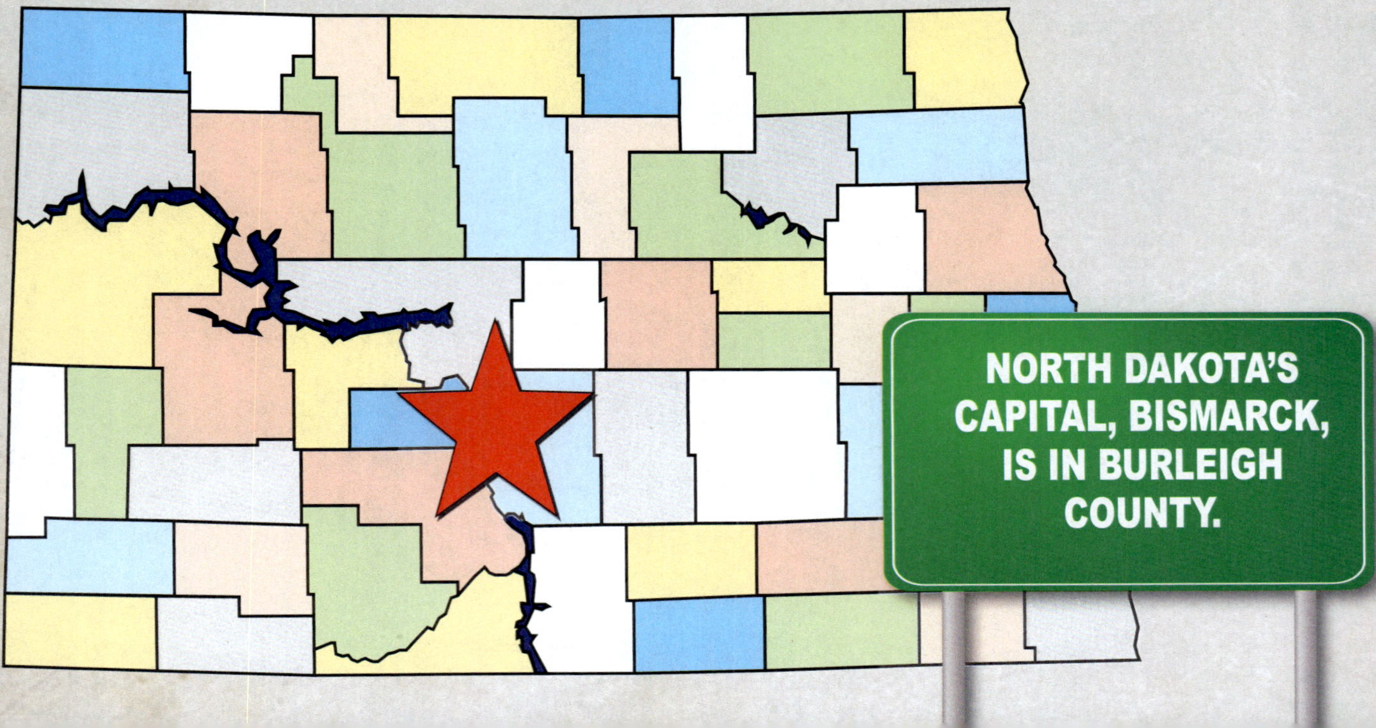

PEOPLE

Many famous people

Sacagawea
Native American who helped Lewis and Clark explore America

Theodore Roosevelt
26th President of the United States

Carl Eielson
First pilot to fly across the Arctic Ocean

call our state home!

PEOPLE

Louis L'Amour
Author of Western novels

Roger Maris
Professional baseball player who broke the home run record in 1961

Monique and Jocelyne Lamoureux
Won silver medals in ice hockey at 2010 Winter Olympics

Western Meadowlark

BIRD

I am the state bird, and I fly
over North Dakota, proud and high.

As I fly, up in the sky,
I flap my wings to tell you "Hi!"

The North Dakota state bird is the
Western Meadowlark.

Wild
Prairie
Rose

FLOWER

I am the Wild Prairie Rose.
I am the state flower.

I grow where it's warm and sunny.
I bloom in spring and summer.
I help make North Dakota beautiful!

Look at me! Smell me!
But don't touch my sharp thorns!

American Elm

TREE

I am an American Elm—I'm the state tree.
All over North Dakota is where to find me.

My roots run deep, they keep me strong.
I can live for hundreds of years—that's very long!

I stand up straight, big and tall.
Don't climb too high—it would hurt to fall!

Ladybug

INSECT

I am the Ladybug
I am the state insect.

I am a type of beetle.
I am red with black polka dots!

Gardeners and farmers love me.
I eat bugs off their plants.
I help North Dakota crops grow.

Great Plains

GREAT PLAINS

Let's go to the Great Plains!

North Dakota has miles and miles of plains.
The Great Plains have soft rolling hills and tall golden grass.
They stretch as far as the eye can see!

North Dakota's Great Plains are home to many animals:

Prairie Dogs **Bison** **Hawks** **Gophers** **Spiders** **and More!**

Badlands

BADLANDS

North Dakota's Badlands are the place to be.
Steep canyons, hills, bluffs and buttes—
It's a beautiful sight to see!

Winter weather brings lots of snow.
Temperatures drop to freezing and below!

The Badlands are located in southwestern North Dakota.

Rivers

RIVERS

North Dakota has many rivers.
People like to use rivers for boating and fishing.

This habitat is home to many animals:

Birds Deer Snakes Frogs Fish and More!

The longest river in North Dakota
is the Sheyenne River.

The Enchanted Highway

The Enchanted Highway is a special road in North Dakota!
Metal sculptures line the highway.
There are sculptures of giant grasshoppers, deer, pheasants, a tin family, and more!

An artist named Gary Greff created the sculptures.
He built them to encourage people to visit North Dakota!

LANDMARK

North Dakota Crops

AGRICULTURE

North Dakota has many farms.
Why?
Because North Dakota has good soil and a mild climate!

Some of the top crops grown in North Dakota are:

Wheat **Hay** **Sunflowers** **Soybeans**

Hey!
Don't forget about me!
North Dakota farmers raise lots of cattle, too.
Mooooooooo!

Sports in North Dakota

Baseball! Basketball! Football! Hockey!
North Dakota has it all.

Whether you like to watch or play,
you are sure to have a ball!

Bison **Fighting Sioux**

Beavers

& More!

SPORTS

North Dakota: Home of Sunflowers

CLAIM TO FAME

North Dakota grows more sunflowers than any other state!
Sunflowers provide us with sunflower seeds and sunflower oil.
They can grow to be 10 feet tall!

Sunflowers grow from about June to September.

GLOSSARY

bluff: a hill with a broad, steep face

butte: an isolated hill with steep sides and a flat top

canyon: a deep valley with steep sides

climate: weather conditions in an area over a long period of time

enchanted: filled with delight or charm

habitat: a place where plants or animals naturally live

laws: rules made by the government

region: an area that has similar characteristics

sculpture: a figure made using wood, metal, stone, or plaster

settlement: the first community in an area